# Unicorn Magic

# Sparklesplash Meets the Mermaids

Daisy Meadows

Special thanks to Jan Burchett and
Sara Vogler

ORCHARD BOOKS

First published in Great Britain in 2019 by The Watts Publishing Group

1 3 5 7 9 10 8 6 4 2

Text copyright © 2019 Working Partners Limited.
Illustrations © Orchard Books 2019
Series created by Working Partners Limited

A CIP catalogue record for this book is available from the British Library.

ISBN 978 1 40835 698 2

Printed and bound in Great Britain by Clays Ltd, Elcograf S.p.A.

Orchard Books
An imprint of Hachette Children's Group
Part of The Watts Publishing Group Limited
Carmelite House
50 Victoria Embankment
London EC4Y 0DZ

An Hachette UK Company
www.hachette.co.uk
www.hachettechildrens.co.uk

# Contents

Aisha and Emily are best friends from Spellford Village. Aisha loves sports, whilst Emily's favourite thing is science. But what both girls enjoy more than anything is visiting Enchanted Valley and helping their unicorn friends who live there.

**Dawnblaze**

Dawnblaze is the Fire Unicorn. She loves to swim in the hot springs on Firework Mountain with her dragon friends!

The Air Unicorn, Shimmerbreeze, is in charge of making sure the air in Enchanted Valley is fresh and clean. She likes to use her magic to create little breezes, so her friends can fly their kites.

Shimmerbreeze

Glitterhoof is the Earth Unicorn, who makes plants grow strong and beautiful. What she likes best is being part of a team – there's nothing she won't do for her friends!

Glitterhoof

Sparklesplash has so much fun playing in the rivers and lagoons of Enchanted Valley. This Water Unicorn wants everyone to love the water, just as much as she does.

Sparklesplash

Enchanted Cottage

Golden Palace

An Enchanted Valley lies a twinkle away,
Where beautiful unicorns live, laugh and play
You can visit the mermaids, or go for a ride,
So much fun to be had, but dangers can hide!

Your friends need your help – this is how you know:
A keyring lights up with a magical glow.
Whirled off like a dream, you won't want to leave.
Friendship forever, when you truly believe.

# Chapter One
# A Riverside Picnic

"Look, Mum!" exclaimed Aisha Khan. "There they are!"

She pointed to three figures appearing at the far end of the sunny little meadow. Aisha took off, feeling the summer dandelions tickling her shins. In a flash, she was standing by the side of Emily

Turner, her best friend.

"My goodness," said Mrs Turner, who stood next to Mr Turner, holding a picnic basket on one arm. "You're a very fast runner, Aisha!"

Emily laughed. "Aisha's good at all sports, Mum!"

"Almost as good as Emily is at science," Aisha replied, smiling. "Come on. My parents are setting up by the river. And

I have a special surprise!"

Emily and Aisha skipped through the grass to where Mr and Mrs Khan waited by a checked blanket laid out in a pool of sunshine next to a sparkling river. Then they watched nervously as the Khans shook hands with the Turners. They hoped their parents would get along as well as they did!

"Pleasure to meet you both," said Mrs Khan. "We love having Emily over at Enchanted Cottage."

"We've heard wonderful things from Emily," Mr Turner replied. "It sounds like an amazing place."

Emily and Aisha glanced at each other. Enchanted Cottage was where the Khans had moved when they arrived in Spellford Village only a few weeks ago. And it *was* an amazing place, from the phoenix statue that stood in the garden to the unicorn door-knocker. It was also a house with a wonderful secret ...

"Look what I've brought!" Aisha said, picking up a piece of tupperware. She opened it to reveal a baker's dozen of brightly iced biscuits shaped like unicorns.

Emily gasped. "They're great, Aisha!"

"They match your keyring," said Mrs Turner. "You girls love your unicorns, don't you?"

Emily and Aisha giggled. If only Mrs Turner knew that the first time Emily had visited Enchanted Cottage, she and Aisha had found a crystal unicorn in the attic. When sunlight had struck the little statue, they'd been whisked off to Enchanted Valley, a wonderful land of dragons, phoenixes and other fantastic creatures who were looked after by a unicorn, Queen Aurora, and her unicorn friends. Queen Aurora had used her magic to create Emily and Aisha's unicorn keyrings out of the crystal one they had found.

The Khans and the Turners were chatting merrily now, and Aisha nodded to the river. "Let's leave them to it," she said, "and explore."

The girls jumped over stepping stones across the River Spell, to where a small waterfall spilled gracefully into a calm, blue pool. As they stared up at it, a sudden beam of sunlight fell around them, making the falling water sparkle like thousands of diamond strands. Emily and Aisha gasped, then looked at each other. At the same time, they reached into their pockets to draw out their unicorn keyrings. Queen Aurora had given them the keyrings so they could get back to Enchanted Valley whenever she called.

As the sunlight hit the crystal unicorns, they lit up in a dazzling show of sparkles.

"You know what this means," whispered Emily.

"Queen Aurora's calling us," Aisha whispered back, excitement bubbling up inside her. "Let's go!"

"We have to hide first," warned Emily.

Aisha turned back towards their parents on the riverbank. "Mum," she called, "can

Emily and I go under the waterfall?"

Mrs Khan exchanged a glance with Mr and Mrs Turner, who nodded. "OK," she replied. "But just for a moment!"

Aisha grinned at Emily as she took her friend's hand and ducked under the waterfall. No time passed in their world while they were in Enchanted Valley. They'd be back before anyone missed them.

The girls found themselves in what felt like a tiny chamber with a cool stone wall opposite the waterfall and a floor made of smooth river rocks. Even through the water, the sunbeam made the rocks shine.

"Ready?" Emily asked.

"Ready!" said Aisha.

They held out their unicorn keyrings
and gently touched the sparkling horns
together. At once the crystal unicorns
glowed even brighter, brilliant blues and
reds and greens swirling inside them.
Then … *WHOOSH!* Their hiding place
suddenly disappeared as they were lifted
off their feet, and a burst of light showered

the girls in twinkling stars. When the stars faded away, the girls felt themselves drifting down at the foot of a high, grassy hill. On the hilltop they could see Queen Aurora's golden palace. Its silver drawbridge glinted in the sun and yellow flowers as big as saucers climbed its walls. Eight spiral turrets like unicorn horns gleamed against the blue sky.

"We're in Enchanted Valley!" the girls chorused in delight.

"Come on!" yelled Aisha, running up the hill. Emily pulled her hair back into its ponytail and followed, enjoying the feel of the soft, sun-dappled grass brushing against her ankles. Soon they were at the top, gazing breathlessly down at the great lush forests, green meadows dotted with blue forget-me-nots, and sparkling lakes that spread out below.

Emily turned towards the palace and spotted a beautiful unicorn standing on the drawbridge that ran over the palace's moat. Her coat shimmered with the pinks, oranges and golds of a perfect sunrise.

"Queen Aurora!" cried Emily happily. The girls flung their arms around the queen's neck and gave her a huge hug.

Atop her head was a silver crown, and
round her neck hung a locket that held
two dancing suns. Emily and Aisha knew
the locket was magic. Each unicorn had
one, and each locket protected something
in Enchanted Valley. As queen, Aurora was
in charge of peace and friendship, and
the suns in her locket looked like two best
friends playing.

"Thank you for coming!" said Aurora in
her soft, musical voice. "It's so wonderful

to see you!"

"You, too, Queen Aurora!" said Aisha. "But why did you call us? Is Selena making trouble again?"

Selena was another unicorn, and every bit as evil as Aurora was kind. And she wanted nothing more than to take the throne for herself. She had already stolen the four lockets belonging to the Nature unicorns, though the girls had managed to get three back.

Aurora nodded and her long golden mane drooped sadly. "We're supposed to be holding the Nature Gala today," she said, "but Selena's been spoiling things. Come and see."

Emily and Aisha exchanged a serious

look. The Nature Gala was a special party the unicorns held every year and all the creatures of Enchanted Valley were invited. The whole kingdom was looking forward to it, and so were Emily and Aisha. They couldn't let Selena ruin it for everyone.

The queen led them through the neat courtyard where small creamy butterflies weaved in and out of the grass, and out

into the lovely palace garden. It was decorated for a party, dotted with tables and tents hung with bunting. Emily and Aisha could tell that the Nature unicorns had been hard at work, using the magical lockets the girls had got back from Selena.

Everywhere was lit with golden sunrays, and from the palace kitchens came the smell of warm cinnamon cakes. The

girls knew that would be thanks to Dawnblaze, the fire unicorn.

Shimmerbreeze, the snowy-white air unicorn, stood by a line of beautifully patterned kites, and with a swish of her horn a gentle breeze swept them up into the air.

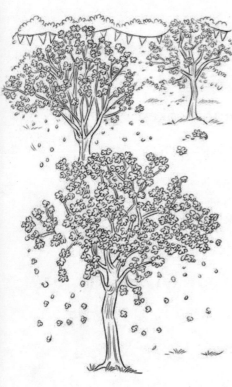

Pink petals fell from the rosy blossoms blooming on the cherry trees and floated on the breeze like confetti. The girls watched as Glitterhoof, the earth unicorn, flicked her horn at an empty flowerbed, and gasped as green stalks came shooting up and sprouted into bright daylilies.

Catching sight of the girls, the unicorns all whinnied and dipped their heads in greeting.

"I wonder what's wrong," Aisha whispered to Emily as they bowed their heads in reply. "Everything seems perfect."

Aurora brought them to a little pool with ivy climbing up its sides. Shining bubbles popped on the surface of its rainbow-tinted water. Sparklesplash, the water unicorn, was peering sadly into the pool, tears rolling down her velvety nose. Sparklesplash was the only Nature Unicorn still missing her locket.

The girls ran to her. "Sparklesplash, are you all right?" Emily asked gently.

"I'm so glad you're here," said Sparklesplash, looking up and nuzzling their cheeks. "I'm trying to make Fizzleberry Surprise for the party."

A big bubble burst beside the girls, showering them with glittery spray.

"It looks fantastic!" said Emily.

"But it tastes horrible," said Sparklesplash, hanging her head. "Try for yourselves."

The girls took two glasses from the side of the pool and had a sip. Yuck! The drink was very bitter.

"Well, it could be a bit better," said Aisha kindly, "but it's not your fault. This is Selena's doing!"

*Zzzapppp!* A bolt of lightning shot from the sky, searing a black mark into the lush lawn. *Ker-rack!* Another hit the party tables. Glasses and plates scattered all over the ground. The unicorns reared in fright. Thunder crashed and a bright silver unicorn burst through a thundercloud above them, sparks flying from her

hooves. Flashes of electricity burst all over her coat. Her locket was full of angry storm clouds. Selena! She cackled as she came to land on the ground, shrivelling the grass beneath her hooves. Her purple eyes set on Emily and Aisha and she gave an angry swish of her twilight-blue mane. "There's no way around it this time, silly girls," Selena said. "Enchanted Valley will soon be mine!"

## Chapter Two
# Selena's Dreadful Plan

"You'll never rule over Enchanted Valley,"
cried Emily. "Not as long as Aisha and I
are here to stop you!"

Before Selena could respond, Flit, her
bat servant, flapped wildly into view.
*Whumph!* He flew straight into a tree.

"I'm sorry, Your Highness," he panted as

he struggled dizzily back into the air.
"I flew as fast as I could."

He suddenly spotted the beautiful
decorations. "Ooooh! Is this a party?
I love a party!"

"Silence!" shrieked Selena. "There's not
going to be a party." Her eyes were lit by
a wicked glow. "The Water locket is still
mine, and this time I'll be sending it to
the deepest depths of the lagoon. And I'll
be sending my best guard down with it!
You'll never see it again!"

"No!" cried Sparklesplash. "Give it back
to me!"

The rest of the Nature unicorns had
come to stand beside Sparklesplash.
They pawed the ground and neighed in

agreement.

"Oh, you'd like it back, would you?"
asked Selena in a sugary-sweet voice.
"Then all you have to do is crown me
queen of Enchanted Valley."

"No way, Selena," declared Aisha.
"Aurora is queen."

"And that's how it's going to stay!"
added Emily.

"We'll see about that, you tiresome

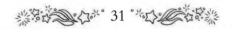

twosome," snorted Selena. "Hold it up, Flit!"

From behind his back, Flit drew Sparklesplash's stolen Water locket, its tiny fountain tinkling inside.

*Gloop!* Thick smoke billowed from Selena's horn. When it cleared the locket was trapped in a floating green bubble. Next, a lightning bolt shot from her horn, sending the bubble flying.

"No!" yelled Aisha. She leaped for the bubble like a goalie after a football, but it spun out of reach and vanished into the sky.

"Bad luck!" scoffed Selena, laughing as

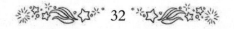

Emily helped Aisha up from the ground.

"Excuse me, Your Great Wonderfulness," said Flit, tapping Selena with a polite claw. "Who exactly is your best guard?"

"You, of course!" said Selena.

Flit puffed himself up importantly, flapping his silky black wings. "What an honour—"

"Because you're my only guard," interrupted Selena.

Flit's ears drooped. "I've just had a teensy-weensy thought, Your Amazingness," he chittered anxiously. "If the locket's at the bottom of the lagoon, how can I guard it? I can't breathe underwater. I'm a bat!"

"You doubt my powers?" shrieked

Selena, stamping her hooves and sending electric jolts zigzagging along the ground. "My magic can do anything! Now come. I've had enough chat for one day!"

With that, she took to the air and zoomed away with a tremendous crash of thunder.

Flit didn't move.

"FLIT!" came an angry shout.

"Eek!" The little bat jumped in fright and flew off after his mistress.

"Oh no," said Sparklesplash. "Look at my Fizzleberry Surprise!"

The drink had turned sludgy-grey. It was bubbling out of the pool and oozing over the grass. The bitter liquid was making the cherry blossoms wilt.

"Look!" cried Aisha, pointing through an archway to the moat. Everyone turned to see the water in the moat churning as it rose steadily higher.

"It's going to overflow!" gasped Aurora, as unicorns leapt into action, trying to clear the party decorations from harm's way. "If we don't stop Selena's magic, the palace will be flooded."

Dawnblaze stared down into the valley.

"Not just the palace," she said quietly, nodding her horn towards a distant lagoon the girls hadn't noticed before. Even from here, they could see that the turquoise water was rising too.

"If the lagoon overflows," said Glitterhoof, her ears twitching with fright, "everyone who lives by it will lose their homes."

"We'll rescue your locket," said Aisha.

"We won't let anyone get hurt," added Emily.

"I knew we could count on you," said Queen Aurora gratefully.

"Hop on my back, girls," said Sparklesplash. "We'll fly to the lagoon right now."

Sparklesplash kneeled down and Emily climbed on behind Aisha. As they both held on tight, the Water unicorn galloped across the soggy grass and took off over the palace wall. The girls heard the unicorns below calling "Good luck!" as they swooped up into the air.

The wind ruffled their hair, and they soared through the crystal blue sky, almost as high as the craggy peak of Firework Mountain. They sailed over the great forest where their friend Hob the goblin lived in his hidden cave.

But as they left the forest behind, they saw Selena's horrid spell at work. In the meadows below, the lakes and streams were spilling over their banks. Worst of all, water came from the vast lagoon and swamped the nearby trees and meadows. Emily and Aisha heard cries of fear as frightened imps and gnomes ran from the flood. Pixies and leprechauns clung to the low branches of trees, but the water lapped at their feet.

"They need help!" Emily cried. "We've got to save them!"

## Chapter Three
# Flood!

Emily and Aisha gazed fearfully down at the swirling waves that were rolling through Enchanted Valley. The forest creatures were standing on the roofs of their houses, calling desperately for help.

"Let's go!" cried Sparklesplash. "We can fly them out."

"Wait," Emily said. "You're only one unicorn. You'd only be able to rescue a few at a time."

"But we've got to do something!" cried Aisha.

Emily thought about it as if it were a science problem to be solved. They needed someone who could fly, and who could carry lots of creatures at once. A memory popped into her head of an earlier adventure in Enchanted Valley – of flying through the clouds.

"Fluffy could do it!" she exclaimed.

Their friend Fluffy was an enormous cloud puppy who'd carried them on his back before and helped them save Shimmerbreeze's Air locket.

"Yes!" cried Aisha.

"That's a great idea," said Sparklesplash. "We'll find him. Hold on tight!" She whizzed up through the clouds.

The girls' keen eyes searched the soft, wispy billows.

"Fluffy!" they yelled. "Fluffy, where are you?"

"Look!" cried Emily. In the distance a giant cuddly cloud in the shape of a puppy was bounding about with a golden ball in his mouth.

Aisha gave a loud whistle. "Here, boy!"

The moment the cloud puppy spotted Sparklesplash and the girls, he sped towards them, a big smile on his soft white face. His huge tail wagged so hard

it sent puffs of cloud everywhere.

"Hello there!" he panted, dropping the golden ball on a cloud in front of them. "Would you like to play fetch?"

"We wish we could," said Emily. "But we need your help, Fluffy, and there's not much time." She quickly told him about the flood, and Selena taking Sparklesplash's locket.

"That nasty Selena," Fluffy growled. "We can't let her win. Don't worry, I'll help. And I'll ask some friends too."

"Thank you!" the girls said gratefully.

Fluffy threw back his head. "Awoooooooooo!" he howled. "Woof, woof, awooooooo! That should do it," he said.

"Wonderful. We'll meet you at the lagoon," Sparklesplash told him. She dived down through the clouds, sending the wind whistling in the girls' ears. As the sky cleared, the lagoon came back into sight. The waters were higher than ever, flooding the valley as far as the eye could see.

"I hope Fluffy and his friends aren't far be—" started Emily.

But just then they heard the sound

of flapping wings overhead. They all
turned to see what looked like a flock of
very large birds swooping down behind
them. As the flock came closer, the girls
made out the shapes of of dragons, cloud
puppies and phoenixes, their flame-
coloured tails streaming out behind them.
Fluffy was leading the charge.

"Great work, Fluffy!" Aisha shouted.
"We're sure to save everybody now!"

A beautiful orange-red phoenix waved a wing at them, the plume on her head wobbling with worry. Emily and Aisha were delighted to see it was their friend Ember. Near her flew six small chicks, chirping to one another as they flapped.

"Hello, my dears," Ember squawked.

"Hello, Ember!" said Emily. "Your chicks are flying!"

Ember smiled. "I'll never forget how you

saved them." The girls and Shimmerbreeze had found Ember's eggs when the nest had been whisked away by Selena's evil tornado. "Now we can all repay the favour."

The girls smiled. The adorable chicks were just big enough to carry a pixie each.

The flying rescue party was soon over the forest. Sparklesplash dived down to land among the trees, where the water covered her hooves. The dragons landed next to her, while the cloud puppies hovered in a nearby clearing so as not to wet their cloud-fur. The phoenixes skimmed over the forest, picking up poor stranded creatures from roofs and trees

and flying away with them.

Emily and Aisha slid off the unicorn's
back, splashing as their feet met the water,
and beckoned to the frightened creatures
who were running from the rising waves.
"This way," yelled Emily.

Imps, goblins, gnomes, leprechauns
and all sorts of forest animals swarmed
towards them. The girls hoisted a
family of dripping gnomes up on to

Sparklesplash's back.

"Can you take them to safety?" Emily asked her unicorn friend.

"Of course," Sparklesplash said, nodding. "I'll be back soon."

Sparklesplash took off. The girls raced over to help a group of elves climb aboard Fluffy's back. They sank, wet and shivering, into the puppy's fleecy coat.

"We're ready to go!" Fluffy announced to his passengers. He took off. "Good luck finding the locket, girls."

One by one, the dragons, phoenixes and cloud puppies rose through the trees. Finally, Emily and Aisha looked around to see that they were the only ones left in the water.

"Phew!" said Aisha. "Everyone's safe."

But something had caught Emily's eye. "Not everyone!" she said. She pointed at the water's edge. A girl was lying in the shallows!

Aisha's eyes widened. They'd never met another girl in Enchanted Valley before.

Ignoring the cold water that surged around them, they raced towards the stranded girl. She wore a crop top made of small white shells and her tangled hair fell in waves of purple, blue and pink around her shoulders. Her eyes were closed and she lay very still, half out of the water.

The water swirled away for a second and the girls gasped. Instead of legs, the

girl had a sleek fishtail that shimmered
with dazzling green scales!

"Wow!" breathed Aisha. "She's a
mermaid!"

# Chapter Four
# The New Mermaids

"Quick, let's get her deeper into the water," Emily said. Aisha took the mermaid's arms and Emily took her tail, and they gently lifted her up.

Just then, Sparklesplash landed among the trees. "Everyone is safe and dry on Firework Mountain," she called. She

gave a whinny of horror as she saw the
mermaid supported by Aisha and Emily.
"Oh, no! What happened to Pearl?"

"We aren't sure," Emily said. "It seems
like she got washed up here."

Sparklesplash watched nervously as the
girls carried the mermaid deeper into the
flood until she was covered in water.

But still she didn't move.

"What do we do now?" cried Emily,
tears pricking at her eyes.

All of a sudden Pearl shuddered. She took a great gulp of air, opened her eyes and sat up. She stared at Emily and Aisha in amazement. Then she noticed the trees sticking out of the water and her sea-green eyes opened even wider.

"What's going on?" she gasped. "Where am I?" Her voice was tinkling and sweet, like a trickling stream of water.

The girls and Sparklesplash explained what was happening, and how they had found her.

"Last thing I remember, I was practising my triple spin for our synchronised swimming routine," said Pearl.

"The mermaids are supposed to be performing at the Nature Gala,"

Sparklesplash told the girls.

"Thank you for coming to my rescue," Pearl added.

Aisha smiled. "Of course! I'm Aisha and this is Emily."

Pearl clapped in delight and gave a tinkling laugh. "I'm so pleased to meet you," she said. "You're famous in Enchanted Valley. You've saved us from Selena's nasty spells. I should have known you'd be here now that Selena's up to her tricks again."

"Can you help us get Sparklesplash's locket back?" Emily asked. "It's hidden in the deepest part of the lagoon."

Pearl shuddered. "The lagoon bed's much too deep for any human to dive to.

It can be dangerous too. Even mermaids don't go that far down alone."

"Then how will we get my locket back?" asked Sparklesplash, a hint of despair in her voice.

Pearl's forehead wrinkled in a frown. "I have an idea!" she said at last. "Wait just a minute." With a flick of her shimmering tail, she disappeared into the waves. No sooner had the girls begun to wonder where she'd gone than she surfaced again, holding out three pretty, shiny combs set with twinkling blue stones.

"These stones are sea sapphires," Pearl explained. "They'll help you swim and breathe underwater!"

Aisha and Emily helped fix a comb
in each other's hair and then placed
Sparklesplash's in her mane.

"But how do they work?" Emily said.

Pearl flashed a mischievous smile.
"You'll see. Come on!" Then she dived
back into the water, leaving hardly a
ripple behind her.

"On the count of three then," Aisha said.
"One …"

"Two …" said
Sparklesplash.

"Three!"
yelled Emily.

The girls and
Sparklesplash
plunged under

the surface. As they did, the water swirled
around them, spinning them faster and
faster. The girls felt a tingling start in their
toes and climb up their legs. When the
spinning stopped, they opened their eyes.
Pearl was smiling at them.

"You look great!" she said.

Emily and Aisha looked down to
see that their legs had turned into
shimmering tails! Emily's was a pearly

pink, Aisha's a deep turquoise.

"We're mermaids!" they exclaimed together.

"And we can talk underwater," said Emily.

"Look at me!" cried Sparklesplash.

They turned to see their unicorn friend floating upright in the water, a new fin on her back and a spindly tail curled underneath her.

"You've turned into a giant seahorse!" said Aisha.

"A sea unicorn!" corrected Emily, pointing at Sparklesplash's horn.

Aisha flicked her tail, gliding through the sunbeams dancing in the water. "Wow! I can swim really well," she said.

"Imagine if your swimming
class could see you now!"
grinned Emily.

"They'd never believe it," said Aisha.

"I knew you'd like it," said Pearl
happily. "Now let's go!"

# Chapter Five
# The Dark Lagoon

Pearl swam off and they sped after her
through the strange underwater world.
As they swam, they grew solemn – they
were passing by tiny villages of flooded
pixie houses, and all around them floated
the pixies' broomsticks, boots and books.
Forest primroses that were usually yellow

and bright wilted in the water. If they didn't manage to find Sparklesplash's locket, none of the creatures would ever get their homes or things back.

Suddenly the ground dipped sharply away, and the girls felt a strong current like an underwater wind pushing against them. Emily stared into the dark depths as she and Aisha grabbed hands.

"Oh, no," Pearl breathed. "The lagoon – it's so different. Usually there are thousands of fish swimming around, and everything's bright and cheery. The water's always perfectly clear."

"Everyone is probably hiding," said Sparklesplash. "The current is very strong."

"But if you want that locket," said Pearl, "there's only one way to go, and that's straight down from here. Stay close to me."

Emily and Aisha took a deep breath. Then they flicked their tails and swam off into the deep.

Down and down they swam. Emily and Aisha held tightly to each other and swished their tails in rhythm to fight the powerful surges of water that were rising from below. *Swoosh!* A shoal of tabby catfish darted underneath them, meowing anxiously as they were tossed in the strong currents. Mermaids peered from the windows of little cottages built into the seabed below. Emily gasped as she caught sight of a brightly glowing starfish fighting to keep its grip on a nearby rock. She reached over and smoothed one of its swinging arms firmly down against the rock's surface. Everyone was struggling against Selena's horrible spell.

Sparklesplash tumbled sideways and used her spiralled tail to right herself. "The currents are growing stronger the deeper we go."

A giant ring of coral came into view below them. It glittered in breathtaking rosettes of green, yellow and pink. Blue bug-eyed frogs and silver sea snails gazed fearfully from every nook and cranny.

"It's beautiful!" breathed Emily. "I wish we had time to explore."

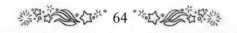

They reached the the coral and peered
over it. Below, the water churned even
more viciously.

"That's where we have to go to find
the locket," said Pearl. "The deepest point
in the lagoon." Her voice was wobbly
with worry. A column of bubbling water
suddenly shot up from the depths.

"What was that?" gasped Sparklesplash,
shrinking back.

"That came from a geyser in the rock,"
said Pearl. "There are lots of them in the

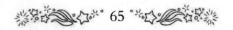

coral ring. That's why even we mermaids don't go there."

"What's a geyser?" asked Aisha.

"It's a vent that shoots up jets of water and steam," Emily explained. "We have them in our world, too."

"Keep your eyes peeled, everyone," warned Pearl. "As soon as you see bubbles rising, get out of the way!"

Everyone took a deep breath and then set off into the coral ring.

But just as Aisha was diving down, she felt something brush against her. She whirled around in the water just in time to see a small, spindly creature shooting past her, squeaking hard as its floppy fins flapped wildly.

"What's that?" she exclaimed.

Pearl's eyes widened as she turned to look. "I've never seen a fish like that in the lagoon."

Catching sight of the fish, Emily saw that there was something very familiar about the creature. It swam almost like it was trying to fly …

"That's no fish," she gasped. "It's Flit! Selena's magicked him into a weird sea creature."

"How rude," called Flit, sticking out his tongue. "You're one to talk, with your scaly fishy tail. Anyway, Selena told me to guard the locket. I'm going to pick it up and hide it somewhere you'll never find it."

With that he flapped awkwardly and plunged into the dark depths.

"Quick!" cried Aisha urgently. "We've got to get the locket before Flit does!"

## Chapter Six
# The Brave Bat

Emily, Aisha and Sparklesplash followed Pearl as she took off after Flit. The inside of the coral ring was different to the rest of the lagoon. The currents whirled them this way and that through the darkness. There were no mermaid homes here, or creatures peeking out at them.

The four friends slowly battled their way down to the craggy lagoon bed, which was carpeted with broken shells and jagged rocks.

"Remember to watch out for the geysers," warned Pearl, "and if you see one starting to bubble, swim away as fast as you can!"

Emily and Aisha peered around the bottom of the lagoon, between sea

boulders and tangled patches of seaweed.
But there was no sign of Flit or the locket.
And it was hard to swim while they were
being thrown this way and that.

"Maybe Flit's already found the locket,"
said Sparklesplash anxiously.

Just then, the current threw Aisha
against a prickly sea cactus. Aisha tried
not to cry out as the thorns scratched
her hands. Then something moved – a

quivering
black shape,
hiding
behind a
sunken log. "Here he is!"
she exclaimed.

Flit squeaked and flapped
hurriedly away. Aisha saw
something clasped tightly in his claws. It
was a slimy green bubble, and the Water
locket was inside!

"He's got the locket!" cried Aisha,
setting off after him.

"Be careful, Aisha!" called Pearl.
"There's a geyser ahead."

Aisha spotted the bubbles rising just
ahead of her and swept her tail sideways

in the water, slowing herself down just in time.

"Phew," she breathed. "Thanks, Pearl. That was close!"

"Aisha!" Emily cried out. "Flit doesn't know about the geysers!"

Sure enough, Aisha turned to see Flit swimming straight into the upward stream of bubbles. With a flick of her tail she rushed forward.

Emily looked on in terror as Aisha grabbed Flit by the fin and pulled him out of the bubbles, just as a powerful jet of water came bursting up from the lagoon bed below.

But Flit had not been able to pull the green bubble clear of the geyser. Before anyone could reach it, the bubble was forced out of Flit's fins and catapulted high out of sight.

"Oh, no!" cried Sparklesplash. "The locket!"

"Oh dear," gulped Flit, round-eyed with fear as he looked up at Aisha. "Selena will be so angry with me! She already made me come here even though I was frightened. What will she do when she finds out I lost the locket?"

Aisha gave the little bat-fish a cuddle.

Emily joined them. "Stay with us, Flit," she said. "We'll protect you."

"But aren't you angry at me for losing the locket?" Flit asked, sniffling.

Sparklesplash nuzzled him with her

nose. "Don't worry," she said. "It's not really lost. As soon as the geyser dies away, the locket will come down again."

Emily suddenly caught sight of a slimy green object above them. "There it is now!" she cried.

Sparklesplash, who was closest, leapt to catch the falling Water locket in her teeth, but before she could, it was whipped away by the current and sank behind a patch of seaweed.

"I'll get it," said Aisha. She swam round the seaweed. "Oh no!" she groaned.

The others rushed over just as the bubble disappeared into a deep, narrow crevice in the rock.

"How can we reach it now?" asked Emily.

"We're far too big to go down after it," said Pearl in despair.

"I'm not!" said Flit. "I'll go."

"Would you do that for us, Flit?" asked Aisha.

"You've been so nice to me," said Flit eagerly. His eyes narrowed. "I thought Selena was nice at first – but she only pretended to be my friend so I'd help with her nasty plans."

"Real friends don't do that," said Emily. "We'll be your friends."

"I'll be yours!" exclaimed Flit, flapping his fins excitedly. He peered down into the dark crevice. "And friends help each other, don't they?"

Flit paused on the edge of the crevice for a moment more. With one of his fins, he saluted his new friends. Then he plunged out of sight.

## Chapter Seven
# Flit's Daring Swim

The girls, Sparklesplash and Pearl all peered down after Flit. The brave bat was swimming deeper and deeper, checking everywhere for the locket.

Then, suddenly, he disappeared.

"Flit, are you all right?" cried Emily in alarm.

There was no
sound from below.

"Do you think
he's stuck?" said
Aisha.

Then they heard a happy chittering. Flit
popped into view with something in his
claws. The bubble!

"Found it!" he called triumphantly.

"Well done, Flit!" cried the girls. Emily
helped him lift the bubble out of the
crevice while Aisha slapped his fin a high
five.

"Now let's get the locket out of this
bubble!" Emily said, pressing the green
bubble down on the tip of a sharp rock
nearby. But instead of bursting open, the

bubble sprang away like a rubber ball.

Aisha caught it and turned it in her hands. "How do you burst a magic bubble?" she pondered.

Sparklesplash gave an excited neigh. "My horn!" she said.

"That's it!" exclaimed Emily. "Your horn is magic, too. Maybe its magic will be stronger than Selena's."

Aisha held the bubble towards Sparklesplash.

The sea unicorn lowered her head and – *SPLAT!* – her horn burst the bubble into hundreds of slimy pieces.

The Water locket floated into Aisha's palm. With Sparklesplash's spiny head still lowered, Aisha quickly looped the locket's silver chain over Sparklesplash's neck. For a long moment, everyone held their breath.

"Did it work?" whispered Pearl.

Then, all at once, the waters became still and calm. The whirling currents were gone. Through the clear water, rays of sunlight filtered down, lighting up the lagoon.

"I think it did!" said Aisha.

"Which means the valley will be safe now," said Emily. "The water should all be drying up."

Sparklesplash nodded. "I think you're

right, girls. Thank you for your help!"

But Flit's nose quivered in fear. "Selena will be furious," he whimpered.

Aisha stroked his head. "We'll protect you," she promised. "Stay close to us."

They swam swiftly upwards. Without the terrible currents, the girls could see the underwater world clearly. The rocks gleamed with encrusted jewels, and rainbow seaweed forests fluttered on either side of them. A school of angelfish passed by, swimming in happy circles, flapping their lacy fins.

The mermaids were starting to come out of their little cottages now, each with a different coloured tail. They waved shyly at the girls as they passed, some of

them blowing kisses, which Aisha caught with a wink.

The group was soon surrounded by all sorts of wonderful creatures – roaring lionfish, barking dogfish and groups of clownfish juggling shells with their fins. Everyone seemed to be coming out to play now that the lagoon was safe again. Then the girls sped upwards and popped their heads out of the gently rippling

water. The flood had vanished from the
forest, which was already looking green
and dry again!

Aisha high-fived with Emily, sending
warm spray high in the air.

"Everything is lovely again," whooped
Pearl. "Thank you, Aisha, Emily and
Sparklesplash. And Flit. You saved the
day."

The little bat grinned shyly. "And I've

made four new friends!" he said.

"Come back to the palace with us," said Emily. "The Nature Gala will be starting soon."

"Yippee!" yelled Flit. "I love parties!"

"We'd better head for shore," said Aisha.

"Or," Pearl said, grinning mischievously, "I can show you a shortcut."

They swam after the mermaid to the mouth of a cave, its entrance hidden by a craggy rock covered in barnacles.

"This way," said Pearl. She dived through the entrance, and the girls found themselves not in a cave but in a secret, underground river! It twisted and turned and soon they saw light up ahead. The river opened up into a wide, sunny pool,

and waiting for them there was a crowd
of chattering mermaids! Their shiny scales
flashed blue, green and pink, and their
long hair billowed round their shoulders.

"Meet my synchronized swimming
team!" Pearl announced proudly. She
clapped her hands and the team dived. A
circle of bright tailfins appeared, waving
hello in perfect rhythm. Aisha joined in.
So did Flit, trying his best to wiggle his
legs just like the mermaids' tails.

"This will be the best party ever!" declared Emily, giggling at the little bat.

"It's probably time for us to get back on dry land," said Sparklesplash.

The girls, Sparklesplash and Flit followed Pearl up to the surface of the water. Blinking in the sunlight, they saw that she had brought them to the palace moat! Emily and Aisha propped themselves up on to the shore and handed Pearl the sea sapphire combs. *Whoosh!* In an instant they were dressed in their shorts and T-shirts and had legs again instead of tails.

Aisha felt a pang. Swimming had been fun as a mermaid. But it would be much easier getting around on land with two

legs! Sparklesplash joined them, a
unicorn once more.

The girls bent down to speak to Pearl.
"Thank you for everything," they said.

"Happy to help!" answered Pearl,
beaming.

"Welcome back!" came a soft, friendly
voice. Queen Aurora and the Nature
unicorns were hurrying towards them.
The unicorns nuzzled them in greeting.
Shimmerbreeze waved her horn over
the girls' heads and at once they were
completely dry.

"We're so proud of you," said Aurora.
"You've saved Enchanted Valley once
again!"

The girls looked around. Everything

had been set up for the party, but there was no one in the garden except the unicorns.

"Where is everyone else?" asked Emily anxiously. "Didn't they all make it to safety?"

Before Queen Aurora could answer, Aisha pointed up to the sky, where a giant flock of creatures was flying towards them, all waving paws, claws and wings as they came in to land. From their backs scrambled the gnomes, pixies, elves and imps. The girls were surrounded by creatures shaking their hands and thanking them for their help. Only one creature seemed to be missing.

"There's someone else who helped us,"

said Aisha. "A new friend. But where is
he?"

"Check out the moat," laughed Emily.

A small black shape flashed by on
its back. Flit was still practising his
swimming!

"We can never have enough friends in
Enchanted Valley," said Aurora, the suns
in her locket shining extra brightly. "Let's

hear it for our brave rescuers. Hip, hip …"

"… hooray," cried all the creatures. Emily and Aisha beamed. The wave of sound surrounded them like a warm hug.

"I must get ready for our display," said Pearl. She slid away under the water.

"And now let the Nature Gala begin!" announced Aurora.

## Chapter Eight
# The Nature Gala

Shimmerbreeze's horn glowed.
*WHOOSH!* Hundreds of balloons rose
magically and danced in the air. Kites
shot up and fluttered in the breeze.
Glitterhoof gave the girls fragrant
flower garlands to wear. Dawnblaze sent
moonpetal muffins flying from the palace

ovens while dragons barbecued fruit kebabs by breathing fire on them.

Sparklesplash led the girls to the fountain. "Try my Fizzleberry Surprise again," she said.

The little round pool gurgled gently. Aisha took a glass. The drink zinged on her tongue, filling her mouth with a glorious taste of sweetness and summer.

"It's delicious," she said.

"And so fizzy!" agreed Emily, giggling

as the bubbles went up her nose.

Emily and Aisha heard a happy chirp
and were delighted to see Ember and
her chicks flying overhead. The flame-
coloured baby phoenixes were playing
fetch with Fluffy. They darted around the
cloud puppy, giggling all the time.

"Hello there!" said a familiar voice.
Their friend Hob was standing there with
Bluebell and Primrose. His
wrinkled face was all smiles
as he handed them each
a pretty blue
flower. "We're
giving everyone
a forget-me-not
so they'll always

remember this splendid day."

"What a great idea," said Emily.

Just then, Aisha spotted something peeking over the garden wall. It was a unicorn, her cold black eyes narrowing as she watched the partygoers.

"Uh-oh!" Aisha whispered to Emily. "Selena's back."

Emily was puzzled. Selena didn't

normally hide. She usually arrived with thunder and lightning. "Do you think she wants to join in, Aisha?" she wondered out loud.

"Let's ask her," said Aisha. "She may have done nasty things, but it would be mean to leave her out. And she might realise that we can be her friends. It's like Queen Aurora said – we can never have too many friends."

"That's a brilliant idea," said Emily. But still, her heart pounded as she and Aisha marched towards the wall.

"Would you like to come to the party, Selena?" called Aisha.

Selena flew over the wall to land next to them. For a moment she gazed at the celebrations, her head on one side. Emily and Aisha looked at each other hopefully. Maybe Selena would say yes!

Then the unicorn's eyes narrowed and she stamped her hoof angrily. "I don't want to come to your silly party. I came to fetch my servant. Where are you, Flit?"

"Coo-ee!" Flit's head popped up from the moat. "I'm having the best time!" he squeaked – until he saw Selena, who gave a furious snort.

"Stop messing around in there!" she snapped.

A flash of lightning shot from her horn and surrounded Flit with smoke. When it cleared he was a bat again. For a moment, Flit's ears drooped as he flapped into the air. "Can I at least stay for cake?"

"No! You're coming home with me,"

Selena commanded in a steely voice.

Flit looked uncertain. Then he caught Emily's eye. She nodded at him and gave a thumbs-up.

"No thanks, Your Great Nastiness," said the little bat, puffing out his chest. "I've made new friends and I'm staying here with them."

Queen Aurora trotted over. "You could stay, too, Selena," she said. "If you

promised not to harm the valley again."

"Yes!" said Aisha. "Try some of Sparklesplash's Fizzleberry Surprise. You'll love it!"

"You think I'd give up so easily?" Selena roared. Sparks flashed around her. "Enjoy your silly party now, fools, because I'll be back, and there will be no stopping me then!"

There was a deafening crack of thunder as Selena turned and flew away.

Ember's chicks gave a little cry.

"Don't worry," Queen Aurora assured them. "We're all safe now."

Emily and Aisha glanced at each other. Queen Aurora was right, for now. But they knew that Selena would be back as she had promised. And when that time came, they would be right here, standing up for their friends.

"The mermaids have a surprise for us," announced Sparklesplash. "Everyone to the moat!"

Selena was soon forgotten as Pearl and her friends began their spectacular synchronised swimming routine. They swam in perfect formation, their arms making graceful movements. Sometimes just their tails showed, swishing intricate figures of eight in the crystal-clear water. At last they all sank under the surface.

"Have they finished?" squeaked Flit in disappointment.

Suddenly Pearl shot out of the water

in a spectacular triple spin. Everyone
clapped. The other mermaids appeared
and caught her, holding her up as if she
were the centre of a beautiful flower.

At that moment, there was a *whooosshh!*
*Whizz! Booooom!* and gigantic red, orange
and yellow sparks shot from the top of the
distant Firework Mountain. As the light
faded, the sky lit up again with exploding
gold and silver stars. There were *ooh*s and

*aah*s from every partygoer until the last dazzling rockets faded from the sky.

Emily and Aisha both gave a yawn as the sky went dark.

"That was a wonderful show, but it's time for us to go home," sighed Emily, turning to Aurora and the four Nature Unicorns.

"We have something to give you before you go," said Dawnblaze.

"It's a thank-you for getting our lockets back," added Shimmerbreeze.

Sparklesplash dipped her horn and – *pzzang!* – two crystal charms in the shape of rainbows appeared in the air, shining with every imaginable colour.

"They're to wear on your keyrings,"

 explained
Dawnblaze.

"They're
beautiful," sighed
Aisha happily.

"Thank you."

"We thought they would remind you of
us," added Dawnblaze.

"They definitely will," said Emily,
stroking Dawnblaze's mane.

When they'd said goodbye to everyone,
Aurora took them into the palace.

"I have something for you," she said.

She led them to the hall of portraits that
the girls had seen before. Pictures of all
the children who'd ever found their way
to Enchanted Valley hung on the walls.

Aurora's horn glowed and a gilded frame appeared and hovered in front of them. It vanished and reappeared on the wall between a boy and girl in frilly white collars and two girls in long satin dresses. Emily and Aisha gasped in delight at the new portrait. It was an amazing painting of them both.

"Now you're in our Hall of Honour," said Aurora. "And I'll be sure to call you again when I need your help."

The girls' hearts were full. They threw their arms around the queen.

"Goodbye,

Aurora," said Emily.

"Thanks for everything," said Aisha.

Then Aurora waved her horn. A cloud of golden sparkles surrounded them and suddenly they were back under the waterfall. The sun was still shining through the water, and they could hear the sound of their parents laughing over the rush of the river. They checked their keyrings. The little crystal charms were still there beside the unicorns.

"What a brilliant party to end our visit!" said Emily.

"I loved the synchronised swimming," added Aisha. Her eyes shone. "Let's ask our parents if we can have a swim in the river. I want to try out some of the mermaids' moves."

Emily gave her a hug. "I'm so glad we found Enchanted Valley," she exclaimed. "I can't wait to go back again."

"Me neither," laughed Aisha, hugging her back. "We've made some wonderful new friends so far, haven't we?"

"Especially each other," grinned Emily.

Clasping hands, the girls ran to enjoy their afternoon by the river.

The End

Join Emily and Aisha
for another adventure in …
## Snowstar and the Big Freeze
Read on for a sneak peek!

Aisha Khan and her best friend, Emily Turner, stood in Aisha's garden, staring up at the grey sky.

"Come on, snow!" they wished together.

The air was freezing cold, and their breath puffed like dragon smoke. They shivered a little, even though they were bundled up in coats, hats and gloves. The grassy lawn behind Aisha's house, Enchanted Cottage, was white with frost, but the air was clear. "It's so cold, I wonder why there's no snow?" said Aisha.

"Perhaps the air is too dry," said Emily.

"It needs to be damp for the ice crystals to form and make snowflakes."

Aisha smiled. "Did you read that in one of your science books?"

"How did you guess?" laughed Emily.

Read

# Snowstar and the Big Freeze
### to find out what adventures are in store for Aisha and Emily!

# Also available

**Book One:**

**Book Two:**

**Book Three:**

**Book Four:**

# Unicorn Magic

## Look out for the next book!

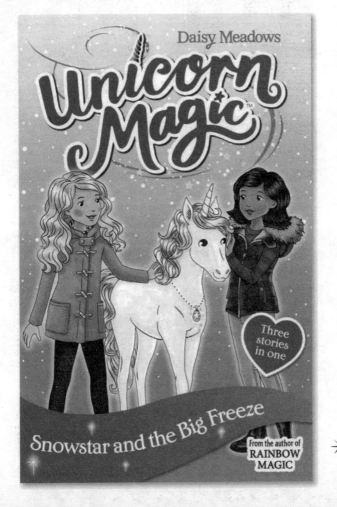

Daisy Meadows

Unicorn Magic™

Three stories in one

Snowstar and the Big Freeze

From the author of RAINBOW MAGIC

If you like
Unicorn Magic,
you'll love …

## Welcome to Animal Ark!

Animal-mad Amelia is sad
about moving house, until she
discovers Animal Ark, where vets look
after all kinds of animals in need.

Join Amelia and her friend Sam for a
brand-new series of animal adventures!